That's What GRANDPARENTS Are For

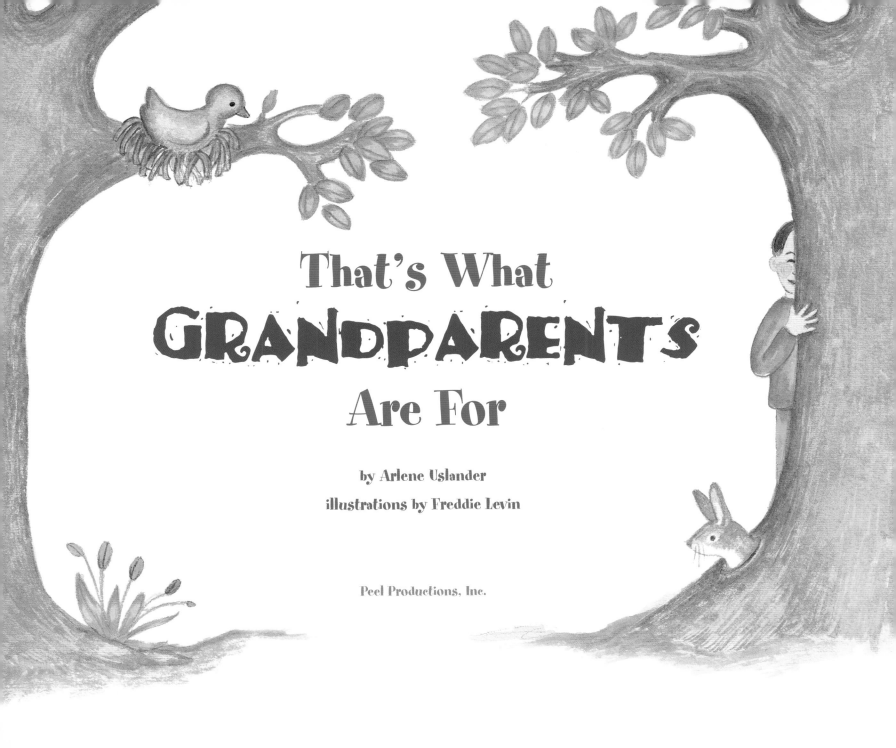

That's What
GRANDPARENTS
Are For

by Arlene Uslander

illustrations by Freddie Levin

Peel Productions, Inc.

*To Eric, Ryan and Carly, and all the
grandchildren everywhere, who have
such a special place in their
grandparents' hearts.*

A.S.U.

For Fanny and Aaron and Betty and Fred.

F.L.

www.peelbooks.com

Text copyright©2002 Arlene Uslander
Illustrations copyright© 2002 Freddie Levin
Al rights reserved.
Published by Peel Productions, Inc.
PO Box 546, Columbus, NC 28722, USA

Printed in Hong Kong

Library of Congress Cataloging-in-publication data
Uslander, Arlene, 1934-
    That's what grandparents are for / by Arlene Uslander;
    illustrations by Freddie Levin. p. cm.
        Summary: Illustrations and rhyming text describe the
    special bond between grandparents and their grandchildren.
            ISBN 0-939217-60-0
    [1. Grandparents--Fiction. 2. Stories in rhyme.] I. Levin,
    Freddie, ill. II. Title.
    PZ8.3.U76 Th 2001
     [E]--dc2 1   2001036641

On the day you were born,
when I first looked at you,
I knew for certain
that dreams do come true.

I cooed and you gurgled,
when I kissed your nose.
I touched all your fingers
and counted your toes.

Whom did you look like?
I tried hard to see.
An angel, of course,
(and a little like me).

To me, you were perfect.
I thanked God above
for giving me you—
a grandchild to love.

You were the cutest baby
(of course, the smartest, too).
I proudly showed your pictures
to everyone I knew.

I bragged about you all the time.
Was I an awful bore?
Perhaps, but after all, you know,
That's what grandparents are for.

When you were just a toddler,
I loved to stay with you.
We'd dance and rock the hours away,
sing songs, play peek-a-boo.

Most times you were the perfect child.
You'd eat your food and clap,
but on those days when you felt bad,
you wouldn't eat or nap.

So, I would hold you in my arms
and we would dance some more.
And I would rock you sound asleep.
That's what grandparents are for.

I took you to the zoo one day;
we had such fun together.
You tried to take a duckling home,
but settled for a feather.

You stroked a baby rabbit.
We touched a white stork's nest.
You laughed to see a seal do tricks,
but liked the monkeys best.

You tried to hide behind me
when you heard a lion roar.
I said, "Sweet child, you're safe with me."
That's what grandparents are for.

You helped me plant my garden
one year as spring arrived.
The earth warmed up and so did I,
for you were by my side.

I dug the holes; you filled them up
with tiny little seeds.
You loved whatever sprouted up,
including all the weeds.

A rabbit liked the carrots,
so he ate quite a few.
You smiled and said, "That's O.K.—
a bunny needs food too!"

You watered all the flowers,
but you watered yourself more.
I dried you off, then hugged you tight.
That's what grandparents are for.

In the middle of the summer,
the circus came to town.
We couldn't wait to see it.
My, how you loved the clown!

We shared some cotton candy,
and then you asked for more.
I let you have another.
That's what grandparents are for!

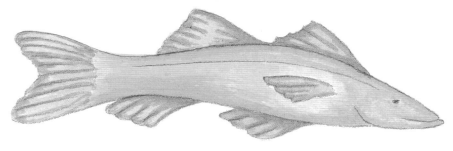

You wanted to go fishing,
so I took you that same day.
You'd never caught a fish before,
but you caught one right away.

When you reeled it in,
you said, "This fish is just a baby!
Do you think its family will be sad?"
I had to answer, "Maybe...."

"Let's throw it back," you said to me,
"and not fish anymore."
"I know just how you feel," I said.
That's what grandparents are for.

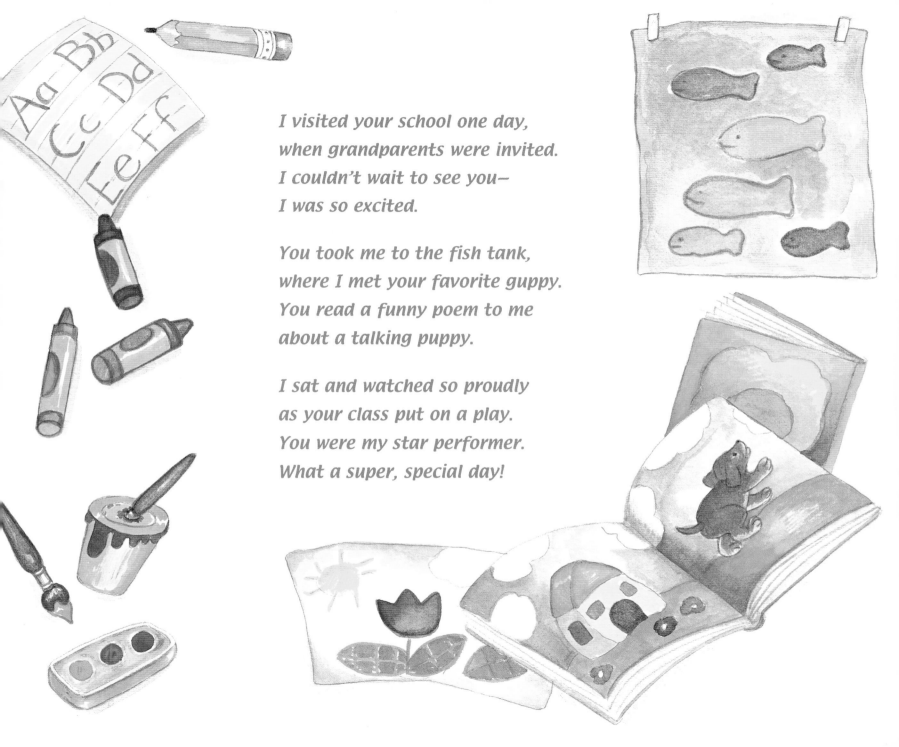

I visited your school one day,
when grandparents were invited.
I couldn't wait to see you—
I was so excited.

You took me to the fish tank,
where I met your favorite guppy.
You read a funny poem to me
about a talking puppy.

I sat and watched so proudly
as your class put on a play.
You were my star performer.
What a super, special day!

One afternoon, we built a kite
and flew it in the park.
We watched it climb up to the stars
as evening turned to dark.

I answered all your questions
about the stars, the sun, the moon.
I told you how a butterfly
breaks out of its cocoon.

You said, "Gran, you're the smartest.
You know everything and more."
"Why, thanks!" I said and smiled at you.
"That's what grandparents are for!"

I took you to the ocean
one glorious summer day.
We watched the tide go in and out
and watched a porpoise play.

We built a great big castle
with buckets of fine sand.
You waved to all the seagulls
whenever they tried to land.

We played until late afternoon.
You wanted to play some more.
And so we played 'til day was done.
That's what grandparents are for.

You wanted a baby brother,
even more than a dog or cat.
But when you finally got one,
you yelled, "Why does he scream like that?"

"He sleeps all day, he's always wet;
he chews my favorite toy.
I'd rather have a puppy
than a brand new baby boy!"

I put my arms around you.
I said, "Hug him when he's sad.
I'm sure that you will like him more,
and then you will be glad."

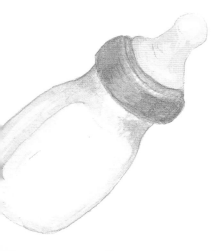

One cold and dreary winter day,
we sat and watched it snow.
You said, "Let's go outside and play."
I said, "Come on! Let's go!"

We built the fattest snowman
and dressed him like a clown.
We built a bigger snowwoman
with a cake pan for her crown.

We made hot cocoa afterwards
and watched the fire roar.
You said, "This was the greatest day!"
That's what grandparents are for.

One weekend we went camping
together, you and me.
We pitched our tent high on a hill
so we could see the sea.

We got up early with the sun
to hike and swim and fish.
At night, we sat beneath the stars;
you made a secret wish.

You said you couldn't tell me yours
or it would not come true.
A long and healthy, happy life
is what I wished for you.

And when our trip was ending,
you said, "Gran, I love you more
than all the stars high in the sky,
than all the times I've asked you why,
than all the fish found in the sea,
than all the leaves in an old, oak tree.
I'll love you for a gazillion years,
and maybe even more."
And then you whispered softly,
"That's what grandchildren are for."